Just Plain Bob

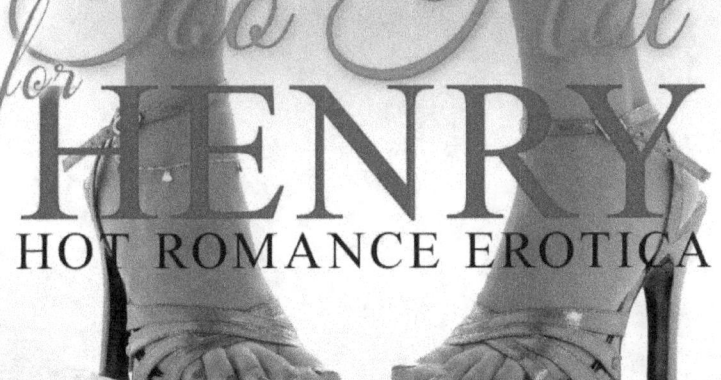

for *Too* *Hot*

HENRY

HOT ROMANCE EROTICA

WARNING

This book contains sexually explicit scenes and adult language. It may be considered offensive to some readers. This book is for sale to adults ONLY.

* * * * * * * * * * * * * * * * * * *

Please store your files wisely where they cannot be accessed by underage readers.

Please feel free to send me an email. Just know that these emails are filtered by my publisher. Good news is always welcome.

Just Plain Bob - **justplainbob@awesomeauthors.org**

About the Publisher

4Fun Publishing, a member of **BLVNP Incorporated**, 340 S. Lemon #6200, Walnut CA 91789, info@blvnp.com / legal@blvnp.com
NOTE: Due to the highly emotional reaction of some people to works of erotic fiction, any email sent to the above address that contains foul language or religious references is automatically deleted by our anti-spam software and will not be seen. All other communications are welcome.

DISCLAIMER

Too Hot for Henry

Hot Romance Erotica

By: Just Plain Bob

© **Just Plain Bob 2014**
ISBN: 978-1-68030-032-1

I got up to go to the bathroom and I noticed that the bedside clock read 3:15. The light from the full moon was coming in the window and it showed her long blond hair fanned out across the pillow. She had kicked the sheet off and the little dangly thing that was pierced in her skin at the navel reflected the light of the moon across her flat stomach as if from a prism. I gazed at her clean shaven pubes and then at the half inch nipples on her 34D cup breasts and wondered how in the hell we had we ended up in bed together.

~~***~~

It started in the tenth grade when my assigned seat in English Composition was right next to Maxine Barber. Maxine, she preferred Maxi, was eighteen going on twenty-five and she wasted no time in letting the rest of us know that we were nowhere near being her equals. She hung with the seniors and was a cheerleader and that made her just so much better than the rest of us lowly sophomores.

Mrs. Harbauer was a no-nonsense teacher and as far as she was concerned, whatever she said in her classroom was 'law' and that was the name of that tune. We were halfway through the semester when she broke the class into teams of two and assigned each team a topic to research and do a seventy-five hundred word paper on. Lucky me, I was given Maxine as a partner. Maxine promptly protested being placed with me and Mrs. Harbauer promptly let Maxine know where the bear shit in the woods.

Well! You couldn't tell Maxine what to do so she solved the problem by not working with me at all which did not bother me in the least because Maxine's attitude toward her peers sucked and I didn't want anything to do with the bitch anyway. So I set off on my own, did the research and started on the paper. The paper was almost done when Maxine found out that the grade on the paper would count as sixty percent of the final grade for the course. No paper meant that Maxine would fail the class and that would lead to her being dropped from the cheerleading squad because of failure to maintain a 'C' average in all of her classes.

Suddenly Maxine decided that not all sophomores were losers and that I just happened to be one of the winners. She came to me and wanted to know what I wanted her to do as her part of the paper. I laughed at her and told her that her name would not be appearing on the paper. I told her that I had done all the work and the paper was three-quarters typed and she could kiss my ass and go back to running with the seniors. That kind of set her back on her heels. She was not used to being told no. She said a few unkind words about my parentage and stalked off.

The next day she was back apologizing and then she asked me what she could do to get her name on the paper.

"You don't have that much money Max."

"I don't like being called Max."

"Tough shit Max."

"Come on Henry, there must be something I can give you to put my name on the paper."

"I don't like being called Henry. I prefer Hank."

She was on the ragged edge of giving me back my "tough shit" when she caught herself.

"How about we go out on a date or two?"

I laughed.

"Come on Hen...Hank, help me out here."

"I have no reason to help you Max."

"Would a couple of hand jobs change your mind?"

I laughed at her again. "You can't be serious Max. I can do that for myself."

"Can you give yourself a blow job?"

"No, but so what?"

"How about head for my name on the paper?"

I did not want to put Maxine's name on the paper, but I wasn't stupid. I was like every other guy my age – I wanted sex! I was not a virgin – hadn't been for two years – but pussy wasn't all that easy to come by when you were eighteen. I'd gotten some, but not near as much as I would have liked. Maxine wanted her name on the paper? I'd just have to find out how bad.

"A blow job won't do it Max. The price is two dates with you to take place on the two days prior to when the paper is due."

Her face lit up and then I gave her the rest of it. "And on both of those dates you will suck my cock and give me your pussy and your ass."

"No fucking way!"

"Okay, your choice" and I walked away and left her standing there and as I walked I wondered what she would do next as the paper was due in one week.

Two days later she was back. "You have me over a barrel Hank. I guess I'll have to do it, but I have something going every night for the next week. How about we do it on the sixteenth and seventeenth?"

I laughed and shook my head no. "Tell me something Max. Why would you want to put your name on a paper prepared by someone as dumb as you think I must be? The sixteenth and seventeenth are a week after the paper has to be in. Once that paper is turned in I have no leverage and when I tried to collect on the debt you would laugh at me and tell me to piss off. It happens before the paper is due. If you have something pressing for the two nights before the paper is due pick any other two days. Just make sure that they are before the paper is to be turned in."

She was looking at me with pure hatred in her eyes and I laughed and said:

"You know what I really should do? I should find out who the next girl on the junior varsity cheer squad to be moved up to varsity is and then see what kind of deal I can cut with her to see to it you get bumped off of the squad so she can take your place. Yeah. I think that's a hell of a good idea. See you around Max" and I turned and started to walk away.

"Okay, okay, you win. Tuesday and Wednesday of next week."

A wise man once said, "When it comes to pussy there is good and there is bad and the worst I ever had was wonderful" and that was true when it came to Maxine. Her blowjobs were half hearted, but I enjoyed them anyway especially since it was Miss Better Than Thou who was giving them to me. She pretty much laid there for the two times I pounded her pussy, but I could tell she was making a huge effort not to give me the satisfaction of seeing her respond. It was a different story when it came to her ass. She got really active when I pushed my way up her dirt road. She yelled and screamed and tried to pull away, but I wasn't about to let that happen. When it was over she said:

"You are a real bastard Henry."

"Hank not Henry. I don't like being called Henry."

"Tough shit. You are still a bastard."

"Maybe, but this bastard will see to it that you get to stay on the cheerleading squad and every game I go to I'll see you there and know that you wouldn't be there if it wasn't for me and you know what? Every time you look up into the stands and see me there you will know it too. You may hate it, but you will still know it."

I turned the paper in and got a B+ on it and it would have been an A if I would have spent the two nights I spent fucking Maxine on proofreading.

~~***~~

The semester ended and I celebrated my nineteenth birthday on the first day of summer vacation. I got a job with a landscaping company cutting grass and I spent my days working and my nights running with my buddies. One night, we were in Harry's Malt Shack and Norm Prince said:

"Did you hear the latest? Maxine Barber is pregnant. She told Dick Spaulding that he was the daddy and he told her to piss off. Then she went to Bert Ellsworth and told him the same thing and he laughed at her. I wonder how many other seniors nailed her and could be the daddy?"

Billy Holbrook laughed and said, "Almost all of them would be my guess."

The next day when I got home from work, I saw my dad's car and a car I didn't recognize in the driveway. I wondered what was up since my dad didn't usually get home that early.

When I went into the house I found my parents and Maxine and her parents sitting there. I started for my room and my father called out:

"Get in here Hank."

I walked into the room and he pointed to a chair and said, "Sit."

I sat down and my dad said, "We have a situation here that needs to be taken care of. The young lady is pregnant and she says that you are the father."

"Bullshit! Oops, sorry for that, but it is garbage. She told Dick Spaulding that he was the father and he told her to get lost so she went to Bert Ellsworth and told him the same thing and he laughed at her. She went to a couple of others and got the same treatment. She has been spreading for most of the seniors for the last year. No way I am the father of her baby."

"Did you have intercourse with her Henry?"

"Yes sir."

"Well she says that you are the father of her child so there it is."

Eighteen was the age of consent in our state so it was as shotgun of a wedding as there ever was and my dad turned the basement into an apartment for us. Our first night as a married couple Maxine said:

"I'm sorry Hank. I didn't want this any more than you."

"Then why did you tell them that I'm the one who got you pregnant?"

"Because they were yelling and screaming at me and all the guys I'd had sex with had told me to fuck off and die and I had to tell my parents something. Besides, it could be yours. The timing is close to being right."

I shrugged and said. "This is totally fucked."

"We will just have to make the best of things Hank," and she started to unbutton my shirt.

"What are you doing?"

"Making the best of things. We have a marriage to consummate."

It was totally different from our first time. She clutched me, pulled me to her, dug her fingernails in my ass, wrapped her legs around me, moaned, begged me to go harder and faster and pleaded with me to make her cum. When it was over she went down on me to get me back up again and her blowjob that time was light years ahead of the first two she had given me. When she had me hard, she pulled me on top of her and we did it again and then a third time.

After that, we did it on the average of twice a night for the next month or so and then it slacked off to once every night and twice a night every once in a while. That part of married night agreed with me. The other part sucked. I had to leave my summer landscaping job and get a full time job at the box factory. Mom and dad gave us free room and board so every cent that I made had to go into the bank against Maxine's coming medical bills. There was no more running around in the evening with my buddies.

Maxine got a part time job at a boutique in the mall and when she wasn't working, she helped mom around the house. Married Maxine was nowhere near where high school Maxine had been. It seemed that being pregnant and having to get married changed her personality one hundred and eighty degrees. When summer vacation was over, I couldn't leave my job at the box factory so I had to settle for going to night school. Maxine held onto her part time job for the weekends, but she went back to school. She stayed on the cheerleading squad figuring that it would be okay for a couple of months.

I was not at all pleased with the situation. I might have only been nineteen, but I was not a brain dead nineteen. Maxine was back in the environment where she had been a punchboard for Spaulding, Ellsworth and several others and now those assholes knew that she was pregnant and they also knew that they couldn't make her any more pregnant and she had been easy before, right? And from Maxine's point of view, it would be pretty much the same. She couldn't get any more pregnant and she had taken care of them before, right? No indeed, I was not a happy camper at all, but there was nothing that I could do about it. Both sets of parents were in agreement that Maxine should stay in school until the last minute and then after the baby was born they would take turns watching the baby until she could graduate. Me? Keep working to provide for mother and child and hopefully get my diploma from night school. Once I had that diploma, my dad said he would get me into the tool and die apprentice program where he worked.

For a month and a half after school started, I barely saw Maxine. I got off of work at five, went home, changed clothes, got a bite to eat and then headed off to night school where I had classes from six-thirty to nine-thirty. Sometimes Maxine was there when I got home from work and sometimes she wasn't because of 'after school activities.' When I got home from school I usually had some homework so our time together consisted of an hour or so before bedtime and the weekends and I couldn't help but notice that our lovemaking slowed way down. This cutback in sex combined with her 'after school activities' and my thoughts of Spaulding, Ellsworth and the rest fed my doubts and one Saturday morning it bubbled over.

I woke up with 'morning wood' and Maxine reached for it. I pushed her hand away and got out of bed. She got up and followed me and asked me what was wrong so I told her.

"I'm tired of putting in fourteen hour days between school and work while you are spending your days at school fucking around with the same guys you fucked around with before. One of whom could very well be the father of the kid that I'm going to be saddled with. What you are doing with them during school and during your so-called 'after school activities' has me so pissed off I could scream, but thanks to you telling your parents I'm to blame and your parents running to my parents, I'm fucked and there isn't anything I can do about it."

She teared up and said, "I don't believe this. You really think I would have anything to do with those assholes after what they did to me? Not that they refused to admit that they were the father, but how they treated me when they did it. Dick told me to piss off and die and Bert laughed and called me a fuck pig and said I deserved to be pregnant and you think I'm seeing them? I'm a married woman now, Hank. I may still be a teenager, but I'm not single any more. As for after school activities? They are part of going to school. You had them too when you were going. I don't know what is bothering you honey, but you have nothing to worry about."

"Then why has our love making gone to pot?"

"We do plenty on weekends."

"What about during the week?"

"You come home so tired from work and school that I don't want to bother you. If you want it all you have to do is let me know."

"I want it."

"So do I!" she said as she reached for my cock.

She convinced me that I was wrong and things went well for a couple of more weeks and then one Friday night I showed up at school and there was a note taped to the door that evening classes had been cancelled so I decided to go to the football game. They were five minutes into the first quarter when I got there. I took a seat and looked at the cheerleaders for Maxine, but I didn't see her. I was sitting next to a couple of my classmates from when I was in regular classes and I asked them if they had seen Maxine that night.

"Not since school this afternoon."

"She didn't come out with the cheer squad tonight?"

"No, but why would she. She quit the squad a month ago."

I felt a cold fist in the pit of my stomach. I looked all around the stands and I didn't see Maxine anywhere. According to Maxine she was still a cheerleader. According to Maxine she had been at last Friday's game cheering on the Red and Gold. Suddenly I had no interest in the game and I got up and left. Maxine wasn't home when I got there and according to mom she hadn't come home from school.

"It's a game night honey; you know she goes right from school to the game."

I gave her a bleak look and didn't say anything. The game should have ended around eight so Maxine should have been home no later than eight-thirty if she intended to keep fooling everybody, but nine-thirty came and she still wasn't home. At ten, the phone rang and my mom answered it. After about twenty seconds she turned to me and said:

"It's the hospital. Maxine has been in an accident."

I hurried down to the hospital and as soon as I got to the emergency room I had to pee so I ducked into the men's room just next to the nurses station. As I came out I heard one of the nurses say:

"I sure hope that I'm not on duty when her husband gets here."

I have no idea why I suddenly stopped and stood where I was, just out of sight of the nurses, but something told me that I would want to hear what was going to be said.

"That wasn't him in the car with her?"

"Not according to the IDs."

"So, why don't you want to be here?"

"You kidding? Hubby comes in, finds wife was in an accident with a man and according to the EMTs on the scene his cock is out, her panties are on the floor of the car, her shirt is open, her bra is off and her boobs are hanging out there in the wind? The last time something like that happened, we had to call the cops to come and restrain the husband."

"So you are saying that we should be somewhere else when he shows."

"You got it."

"What's his name? Who should I be looking for?"

"Wilcox, Henry Wilcox."

I stepped out of the doorway to the john and said, "Too late ladies; I'm already here, but you won't need the cops. Is she alive?"

"Yes, Mr. Wilcox."

"Is she going to stay alive?"

"You will have to ask the doctor that."

"No I don't. You know and I know you know. Tell me what is going on and I'll walk out of here with no fuss."

They looked at each other and then the older one said, "She will be all right, but she lost the baby."

I picked up a piece of paper and a pen and wrote a short note. It said:

"Don't bother bringing your cheating, lying ass home," and I signed it and asked the nurse to give it to Maxine. Then I walked out of the hospital.

Of course, that was not the end of it. I don't know if the nurse gave Maxine the note or not, but Saturday I got a call from Maxine asking me why I hadn't come down and when I didn't answer, she asked me to come and get her.

"Walk, hitchhike, or get whoever picks up the guy you were with last night to give you a ride to your parents' house. You aren't coming back here. I'll put all your shit out on the driveway and your dad can pick it up," and I hung up on her. Twenty minutes later the phone rang and my mom took the call. She covered the mouthpiece with her hand and said:

"Its Maxi's mom. She said you told Maxi you wouldn't pick her up and that she couldn't come home."

"I did and I meant it. She can go live with her parents or the guy she was cheating on me with, but she isn't coming here."

I got up and left the room. About two hours later, I was in my basement room working on some homework when my dad came down and asked me to come upstairs. I came up and found Maxine and her parents sitting on the living room couch. My dad went right to it.

"What is this nonsense about you not going to the hospital to get your wife and where do you get off telling her she could not come back here? In case you have forgotten, this is not your house and you do not get to issue the orders around here."

"Okay. So what have all of you planned for me this time?"

My mom jumped in with, "What is wrong with you Henry? Your wife was in an accident and she is hurting. How can you be so cold to her?"

"I'm glad you asked." I proceeded to tell them everything that I'd found out at the game and at the hospital. "You all ganged up on me and railroaded me last time, but it isn't going to happen again. She is running around just as she did before we were forced to get married and even though I'm not even twenty yet I do know that I do not have to put up with a cheating wife."

I turned to my dad and said, "You are right. This is your house and you get to make the rules, but she is not living with me any more. You bring her back into this house and I'll move out. If she needs a place to live it can be with her folks or with the guy whose car she was half naked in last night, but she is not living with me."

Her dad started to get up off the couch saying, "You can't call my daughter names like that."

"I damned sure can. I told you back when you ran me through that shotgun wedding that she had accused half of the senior class of being the father of the baby she managed to lose last night while she was out cheating on me. She was a whore then and she is a whore now. All you have to do is check the EMT and police reports on her accident and a call to the school can verify that she quit the cheer squad a month ago. A month ago! A month of her telling us that she has been going to the games and cheering every Friday night when she isn't here. I'm not making any wild accusations here. You can check on everything I've said and see for yourself."

He sat back down, turned to Maxine and said, "Is any of what he is saying true?"

"No daddy. I didn't quit cheer squad. They dropped me because I was slowing down because of my pregnancy, but I told everyone I was still on the squad because I felt guilty for letting them down so I kept quiet about it."

"So, where did you spend your Friday nights?"

"I still went to the games."

"And your after school activities?"

"I was working with the girls on the JV squad helping them get ready to move up to varsity."

"And Friday night?"

"I got sick during the game and Ralph offered to give me a ride home. We were on the way when some drunk hit us."

Maxine's mom said, "See Henry? There is a perfectly reasonable explanation for it. I think you owe Maxi an apology."

"I don't believe you people. She lies through her teeth and you tell me to apologize. First, I was at the game Friday night. I got there just after the first quarter started and I looked all over for Max and she was not there. I sat with Donny, Paul and Bev and they told me that Max had quit the cheer squad and had not been to a game since quitting. Secondly, the accident she was in happened at Thornhill and Martin Drive which is ten miles west of the school. In case you have forgotten, we live six miles east of the school. That is a hell out of a way to be coming home from the game sick. Lastly, there are the EMT and police reports."

I was fudging on that since I hadn't seen the reports either – if there even were any reports at all – and I was just going on what I'd heard from the nurses.

"We are expected to believe that the impact of the accident was so hard that it made Max's panties fall off of her and land on the floor of the car? The hit was so hard that it made Max's shirt come unbuttoned, her bra to unsnap, and release her breasts out into the open? The collision caused Ralph's pants to unzip and his penis to jump out? Yeah! I can see how that might happen."

I looked around the room at everyone and then said, "I don't care what you do with her cheating ass. Just keep her away from me," and then I walked out of the room and went back down to the basement. Ten minutes later my dad came down and told me that Maxine was going home with her parents and that Monday he would check around and find a councilor that Maxine and I could sit down with to try and work things out. He obviously wasn't going to pay any attention to whatever I said so I just nodded my head and said nothing.

Monday after work, I stopped at the bank and took out all the money I had been saving to take care of Maxine's and the baby's medical expenses and then rented myself a room at Bailey's boarding house. Tuesday, I took half a day off work and moved all of my things to the boarding house.

It took three days for my dad to figure out that I had moved out and wasn't coming back and I found him leaning on the fender of my car when I got off work on Friday. He told me how disappointed he and my mother were in me because of my failure to accept my responsibilities as a husband and then I told him how disappointed I was in him for not listening to a word I'd said.

"She is a whore and a cheat. She has always been a whore and I am done with her. If you and mom can't accept that then go on home and leave me alone and I'll make sure to stay out of your way so you don't have to look at me and feel disappointed."

I got in my car and drove off leaving him standing there.

For the next four months, I went to work, went to my night classes and hung out with my buddies on Saturday nights, I never saw Maxine or heard anything of her, but then I wasn't asking about her either. I never heard a word from my parents so I didn't bother contacting them. Why remind them that they had a son they were disappointed in.

Just before spring break I was served with divorce papers and I tossed them in the trash without reading them. I kept working and going to night school and then it was June and my eighteenth birthday. I had enough regular and night school credits to take the test for my GED so I took the test and then I took my birth certificate and GED certificate down to the recruiting office and three days later I was on the way to Fort Knox, Kentucky to begin basic training.

~~***~~

I served my three years and then let myself be talked in to reenlisting for three more and pretty close to the end of my second enlistment – just when I was contemplating going for twenty – a new lieutenant was assigned to our unit. The man was a flaming asshole and for some reason he picked me to pick on. I received two Article 15s in a six-week period and when the first shirt called me into his office and handed me the reenlistment papers, I handed them back and told him no way. He tried to talk me into signing and told me that Lt. Mullins wouldn't be around forever and then I pointed out that Mullins had already given me two totally underserved Article 15s and if I stayed in, all I had to look forward to was a summary courts martial or worse. Mullins would be around for at least a year and that would be more than enough time for him to railroad me into Leavenworth.

"Thanks top, but no thanks."

My last night on post, I snuck over to the BOQ and poured sugar in Mullins gas tank and the next day I was riding the big gray dog on my way home.

~~***~~

I found a job at Wayman Industries in the shipping and receiving department and in six months I was the loading dock foreman. One year later, I was chosen to fill the manager's slot. It helped that my Army time was spent in the Quartermasters and moving and handling material was what I did. I was able to find a civilian computer program that I was able to adapt the Army's inventory control program to and that saved Wayman's a lot of time and money.

When I got home, I hit all of my old haunts and reconnected with some of my old buddies and started getting together with them on Friday and Saturday nights. One day, I ran into my uncle Ray in Wal-Marts and he asked me if my parents knew that I was back in town and I told him probably. Two of dad's lodge brothers worked at Wayman and they had more than likely told dad that I worked with them.

"Aren't you going to get in touch with them?"

"Probably not. Don't want to remind them of the irresponsible son they were so disappointed in."

"That was years ago, Hank."

"Maybe so Uncle Ray, but they have made absolutely no attempt to talk with me since I walked away from Maxine. They want to talk to me they know how to do it."

He shook his head and walked away.

~~***~~

It was a Saturday night and I was at Riley's Roadhouse waiting for a couple of friends. I was sitting at the bar watching the TV mounted up on the wall and nursing a Pabst Blue Ribbon when someone took the stool next to me and a voice said:

"Buy a girl a drink?"

I looked over and saw Maxine. She looked damned good and as I was looking at her and wondering what to say, the bartender set a vodka tonic down in front of her. She smiled at me and told the bartender to put it on my tab. He looked at me and I shrugged and nodded a yes.

"How have you been ,Hank?"

"Pretty much okay, Maxi."

"That's the first time you've ever called me Maxi."

"It is the first time I've heard you say Hank without a sneer in your voice."

"Can we take a booth and talk?"

I didn't see any of the guys I was waiting for so I said okay and we moved to a booth. We sat down and she said:

"You are looking pretty good."

"You aren't looking to shabby yourself."

"No sense beating around the bush here so I'll get right to it. I'm sorry for what happened."

"Sorry for doing it or sorry for getting caught?"

She smiled at that and said, "A little bit of both." She hesitated for a moment and then said, "No, this is a time for honesty so make that seventy thirty with the seventy being the sorry for getting caught."

"So why did you do it?"

She sat there quiet for a bit and then said, "I did it because I was young and dumb. I did it because I was rebelling."

"Rebelling? Rebelling against what?"

"Against being in the situation I was in."

"I don't understand that."

"I didn't want to be married any more than you did Hank. I was forced into it the same as you were. My parents may have acted like they didn't think their little girl was a slut, but they knew the truth. I went to them, told them I was pregnant and asked them to help me get an abortion, but they refused. They made me tell them who I had been with and then they went to the parents of the guys I'd named and the guys admitted to screwing me, but said no way the baby was theirs and their parents stood behind them and told my parents to take a hike. You were the last name on the list and I hoped that your parents would stand behind you like the other parents stood behind their sons and that would force my mom and dad to arrange for the abortion, but your parents caved and we were forced to get married.

"It was just wrong, Hank. We had nothing to build a marriage on. I didn't love you and you didn't love me. All there was to cement us was a baby that we both knew only had a one in seven chance of being yours. I liked you Hank. I liked being able to make love to you every night and for what it is worth, none of the others was any better than you. I liked the way you stepped up even though you doubted that the baby was yours, but although I liked you I didn't love you. I did love screwing around and I loved making it with other guys.

"I was a slut, Hank and I loved being a slut. I wasn't ready to stop being a party girl and go into a life where I could only have one man. I managed to be a one man woman for five weeks after we were married and then I was back to being what I was before I got pregnant. Actually, it was better because I got a kick out of cheating on you and there was no shortage of guys who wanted to screw the married pregnant slut. A couple of guys were already planning a gangbang for me when I got to my eighth month and I was telling them who I wanted there and then that accident happened and everything went to shit. You walked, my parents pretty much became jailers until I graduated, got a job and moved into my own place. What about you? What have you been doing?"

I told her about my time in the service and my job at Wayman. About then, the guys I was waiting on showed and I told Maxi I had to go join them. She took a piece of paper out of her purse, wrote on it, handed it to me and said:

"Call me."

I looked at the paper and saw that it was a phone number. I put it in my pocket and went to join my friends. I forgot about that piece of paper until I found it while doing my laundry. I looked at it for a few seconds, then muttered "nah" and tossed it into the wastebasket with the lint from the dryer's filter.

~~***~~

The next year flew by. The job was going well. I was dating a lot, getting laid a lot and even had two fairly long term relationships – long term if four months can be considered long term. I found a small three-bedroom house with a two car attached garage that I could afford and I took on a thirty-year mortgage. I turned one of the bedrooms into a home office and den and started spending my weekends improving the place.

I saw Uncle Ray every so often and he always asked if I'd seen my parents and I always said no. He kept telling me that I needed to talk to them and I kept telling him they knew where to find me.

It was another Saturday night and I was at Riley's Roadhouse with two guys I worked with. Tom and Phil were sitting across from me in the booth and I saw both of them suddenly look past me and smile just as I felt a tap on my shoulder. I turned and saw Maxine standing there. The reason for Tom and Phil's smiles was obvious. Maxine looked drop dead gorgeous.

"You haven't come over and asked me for a dance so I decided to come to you."

She extended a hand and I said to myself, "Why the hell not," and I got out of the booth and we moved out onto the dance floor. A waltz was playing and as I took her in my arms for the very first time on a dance floor she said:

"You never called."

"What would be the point?"

"Who knows? It was years ago Hank and I was a wild dumb bitch then. I've grown up since then. You might even like the me I am now."

"Yeah! Right! I can see it now. I take you out on a date and your dad comes looking for me with that shotgun again."

"No fear of that. Dad was killed in an auto accident about a year after you left."

"Sorry to hear that. How's your mom getting along?"

"Good I guess. I haven't talked to her in a while. She remarried two years after dad died and she and her new husband moved to Canada."

I couldn't think of anything to say to that so I changed the subject. The song ended and she asked me to join her and I begged off saying that I was with friends and we had plans for the evening. She gave me a disappointed look and then said:

"Call me Hank, please?"

"I didn't keep your number."

"I'm in the book."

"I don't know your last name."

"Sure you do. You gave it to me."

I took her back to her table and was halfway back to my booth when her "You gave it to me" hit me. She still had my last name! That was something to think about. I would have thought she would have gotten rid of it and gone back to her maiden name. Then something else occurred to me. If she still had my last name, it would seem that in the eight years since I walked out of my parent's living room leaving her sitting on the couch she had never remarried. Why not? She was gorgeous. She had to have at least half the single guys in town after her (and probably some of the married). Curious. Curious indeed.

When I got back to the booth Phil asked, "Who was that fox?"

"My ex."

"You had a girlfriend like that and you let her get away?"

"Wife."

"What?"

"Not ex-girlfriend, wife."

"That's even worse. I have to seriously question your judgment and sanity son."

"Looks aren't everything Phil. Remember that. Words to live by."

~~***~~

Of course, I thought about the things I'd thought about and curiosity being what it is it hung around and finally got to the point where I wanted to find out the answers. I didn't know any of Maxine's current friends and I couldn't think of any mutual friends that we might still have so the only way I was going to find any answers was to talk to Maxine and that meant calling her and asking her out.

Did I really want to do that? Was I really that curious?

I looked her up in the phone book and gave her a call.

I was there to pick her up at six sharp and she asked me in. She apologized for not being ready to go, but her baby sitter was running late.

"Baby sitter?"

"Well sure. I can't leave Merrily here alone. She's only seven."

"Oh. I didn't know that you had gotten married again."

"I didn't."

"Oh."

Jut then the doorbell rang and it was the sitter. Maxine told her that Merrily was in the bathtub and to make sure that she was in bed by nine and we left. The plan for a night was dinner and a show. After dinner was over and we were having an after dinner drink Maxine said:

"Go ahead, Hank"

"Go ahead."

"It is written all over your face. You are dying to ask questions so go ahead and ask."

I sat there trying to think of what to say and Maxine said, "Okay, I'll start the ball rolling. Merrily is seven going on eight and I am a single mom, but not by choice. Her father couldn't marry me so he finally packed up and left."

"He couldn't marry you? Why, was he already married?"

"No. I was"

"You remarried a guy with the same last name as mine?"

"Not exactly."

"I'm confused."

"Think about it Hank. He couldn't marry me because I was already married. I haven't remarried and I still have your last name. Put the pieces of the puzzle together Hank."

I sat there staring at her as what she was getting at finally dawned on me. "You can't be serious. I saw the divorce papers. You had them served on me."

"But you never signed them and sent them back."

"No way Maxi; no way are we still married."

"Way Hank. You never signed the papers and daddy, who was paying for the divorce, died and I couldn't afford the lawyer by myself so things sort of petered out. By the time I had a decent enough job and was making enough money to go back and pursue the divorce, Merrily came along and I suddenly had more important uses for the money. Being a single mommy means you have to budget and a divorce was way down on the list of priorities. I have a question for you. Did you ever get married again? Did you unknowingly commit bigamy?"

"Thank God no! I came close once, but never did it. Damn. This does complicate things."

"Why? It just means that if you ever decide to get married again you will have to divorce me. Until then it doesn't really matter."

"What about you? What if you want to get married again?"

"I'll cross that bridge when I come to it. The line in front of a single mom's door is never very long and it is even shorter when the single mom has a reputation."

"You still doing that?"

"Good God no. I finally woke up to the fact that it was self-destructive behavior, but the town isn't all that big and people have long memories. I never lack for dates. Guys are always asking me out hoping that I'm still the same old Maxi, but most of them end up disappointed."

"Most of them?"

"Don't act dumb and surprised Hank. I may not spread it around like I used to, but I still have needs. How about you Hank? Do you have needs?"

I just looked at her because, quite frankly, I was at a loss for what to say. She reached across the table and touched my hand and said:

"We can skip the show and go to your place." She giggled and then said, "After all you are my husband and husbands do have certain rights."

She was every bit the sexual athlete she had been the night of our wedding, which is to say that she was fucking insatiable. As fast as I came, she was on it working to get it up again. Fortunately, for me it had only been a couple of days since I'd last gotten laid or my first time could have measured in seconds. She managed to get it done three times, which was no mean trick given she only had three hours in which to get it done.

I had her home by midnight and at her door she kissed me long and hard and said:

"Don't forget hubby dear, you have rights so call me….soon, okay?"

I drove home in a highly confused state. I was still married to Maxi? Could it really be true? Then I remembered that I had dropped the divorce papers unread into the trashcan. If I was supposed to sign them, I never did. Now what the hell should I do? When I woke up the next morning, I had no better idea than I'd had before going to bed, but one thing I did know; pussy was pussy and as pussy, Maxi was head and shoulders above what I'd been getting since I got home. I was going to take advantage of the fact that she had told me that I had 'certain rights.'

I called her Monday and we had dinner and ended up at my place. I had something to do Tuesday night, but I made a date for Wednesday. When I picked her up, I met Merrily for the first time. She shook my hand when Maxi told her to, but she didn't smile and when I tried talking to her she scooted over next to Maxi and hugged her leg while staring at me. When we left, I asked Maxi where she would like to go and she said:

"Your place."

"I don't have enough in the fridge to make dinner."

She laughed and said, "You never used to be this slow Hank."

"Oh. Oh yeah. Of course. My place. We can go to my place."

When we got there, Maxi headed straight to the bedroom and she was half undressed by the time I got there. Remembering the past with Maxi, I had loaded up on condoms and hoped that I hadn't been unlucky on Saturday and Monday. Maxi watched me take a condom out of the bedside stand and told me:

"You wasted your money Hank. You won't need those with me."

"Oh yes I do. I seem to remember a wedding because I didn't use one."

"That was then Hank. There were complications when I had Merrily. There are no babies in my future."

I dropped the condom back in the drawer and climbed on the bed and moved between Maxi's spread legs.

~~***~~

Over the next six months I spent more and more time with Maxi, but one thing never changed. Merrily would always say hello to me, but only when Maxi told her to. I mentioned it to Maxi and she told me that Merrily wasn't used to being around adult males and that eventually she would come around. I would take Maxi and Merrily out on a Saturday or Sunday, but the kid always stayed as far away from me as possible. And I never – not once – got a smile from the kid.

One night when I was having dinner at Maxi's place, she seemed down in the dumps and I commented on it.

"It's my job. I like the work, but I don't like the people I work for and I can barely stand the people I work with."

"So leave and get another job."

"It isn't that simple. If I leave ,I lose my health insurance."

"So? Find a new job where they have health insurance."

"I'd be without insurance while I was looking and then when I got a new job, there would be a waiting period before I would be eligible to sign up for coverage. With a daughter Merrily's age, you can't be without medical insurance unless you have deep pockets and I don't."

When dinner was over, we played cribbage – no hanky panky because Merrily was in the house – and then I kissed her goodnight and headed home.

To this day, I do not know why I did what I did considering that it was for a kid that didn't like me, but I called Maxi the next morning and asked her to meet me for lunch. At lunch, I told her if she as willing to tell a couple of small lies I could help her out with her insurance problem.

"How can you do that?"

"We are still legally married, right?"

"Yes."

"So I can put you on my health insurance at work. All I have to do is say that we were separated and going for a divorce and that you had insurance where you worked so I had never added you to mine."

"You said a 'couple' of lies. What is the other one?"

"We have to say that Merrily is our daughter."

"Can we get away with that?"

"I don't see why not. We are married and can produce a marriage license if they ask for it. The only problem we might have is if they ask for Merrily's birth certificate."

"Why would that be a problem?"

"It will have her father's name on it."

"So?"

"It will have the name of the guy who got you pregnant down as the father."

"No, it won't."

"Why not?"

"Because by the time Merrily was due to pop out, he was already in the wind and I knew he wouldn't be back. I didn't want his name on the birth certificate and I wasn't going to put down 'father unknown.' I never expected to see you again so I put your name down so that her birth certificate would match the marriage license."

I just looked at her for a bit and then asked, "Were you ever going to share that with me?"

"I hadn't planned on it. I saw no need to. I didn't expect that you and I would ever be in a position where you would need to know. Why are you suggesting this?"

"It will cover you while you are looking for another job."

"I know that, but why are you doing it?"

I had to consider that for a moment before truthfully answering, "I don't know. It just seems like the thing to do."

If I had stopped to think it through the outcome was predictable. Maxi and Merrily went on my insurance; Maxi quit her job and found a better one and six months later she and Merrily were living with me.

~~***~~

Maxi and I did much better the second time around. Maxi fell into the role of working wife and mother as if it was designed for her, but the relationship between Merrily and me remained cool. It didn't help any that the first time I had to get after her for making a mess and not cleaning it up she hit me with:

"I don't have to do what you say; you aren't my father."

Maxi quickly straightened her out, but all that did was make her resent me for getting her in trouble with her mother. Merrily and I never did bond on any level and as she got older she got a little more rebellious where I was concerned. She was openly defiant whenever Maxi wasn't around and I gave up going to Maxi about it.

One day, when Merrily was fourteen, she sassed me over something that I can't even remember and it was the proverbial "one time to many" and I lost it and gave her an open handed slap across her mouth and told her that I was not going to put up with any more of her shit and that as long as she lived in my house she would damned well behave.

Three weeks later, I caught a boy climbing into her bedroom window. Maxi had finally had enough and she committed Merrily to the Mount Airey Psychiatric Center in Denver. It was almost five months before Maxi would sign off on letting Merrily be released and only then because Merrily's caseworker said she had seen major improvement in Merrily's behavior.

Three weeks after her release, she ran away. It took the cops a month to find her and one month after that she was gone again. It took three months to find her that time. Personally, I had hoped that they never would. Two months after her return, she told Maxi that she was pregnant. By then, she was over eighteen, which was the age of consent where we lived. The boy she said was the father was seventeen and he owned up to it and said he was glad because "now she has to marry me." They both wanted it so Maxi let it happen and Merrily and her new husband moved in with his parents.

We found out later that Merrily wasn't pregnant. It turns out that she and the boy had made up the story so the parents would let them get married. Maxi wasn't all that happy about the way she had been played, but I could not have cared less. The troublesome little bitch was out of my house and life and that is all I cared about.

~~***~~

All of the shit with Merrily wasn't the only problem I had. My Uncle Ray kept asking me if I'd talked to my folks and I kept telling him no and that if they wanted to talk to me they could find me easily enough. It finally reached the point where I told him if he didn't get off of the subject I wouldn't even talk to him any more.

Another thing was that about five years after Maxi moved in with me, I began to suspect that she was cheating on me. I didn't see any of the so-called obvious signs, but I still suspected. I didn't have much to go on. All I had was a feeling. She just didn't 'feel' right if you know what I mean. I mean I know what she felt like when we made love, but all of a sudden it didn't feel 'that way' anymore. It didn't 'fit' as snug or at least I didn't think it did. It felt a little bigger, as if something larger had just been there, or maybe something the same size had recently been there and she hadn't tightened back up yet. I'm probably putting it down wrong, but what it amounts to was just that I 'had a feeling.' That feeling, coupled with my knowledge of her behavior back when we had gotten married started me watching her closely to see if I could come up with anything factual to back up that feeling.

A couple of years went by and I never came up with anything. I even followed her a couple of times. I thought about hiring a private detective until I found out what it would cost. It would have been reasonable if I knew for sure Maxi was cheating and all I needed was proof I could use, but what if I was wrong? What if my 'feeling' was just me being insecure – not that I thought I was insecure. If I was wrong, the detectives could have followed her for days, weeks or even months with nothing happening except that the meter would still be running. Nope! No way could I afford that.

There was no change in Maxi's behavior toward me. She was affectionate, attentive and our lovemaking held steady at three or four times a week. I had no complaints. All I had was that stupid 'feeling.'

~~***~~

The years slipped by and one day I came home from work and saw Merrily's car in the drive. I debated just driving on by and going to a bar to drink beer and kill time until she left, but then decided that I could just go down in the basement and work on the book case I was making. As I pulled in and parked, Merrily and Maxi came out of the house and got stuff out of Merrily's car and Merrily carried what she had into the house as Maxi walked over to me. Before I could ask her what was going on she kissed me on the cheek and told me that dinner would be a bit late.

"I'll start it as soon as I get Merrily moved back into her old room."

"Moved in to her room?"

"She caught David in bed with the next door neighbor and she left him."

"The next door neighbor? They live next door to a couple of guys."

"Yes, indeed."

"Oh," I said as the light bulb came on above my head.

"Don't worry baby; it will only be until she can find a job that will pay enough for her to get a place of her own."

"Right," I thought to my self, "And just how likely is that for a twenty year old that dropped out of high school when she got married." I just shrugged, got a beer from the fridge and headed for the basement. A month went by and Merrily and I avoided each other as best we could and then one day her moving back in paid dividends.

Before hearing aids were invented, deaf people used to use a small funnel held up to their ear to help them hear better. In our house, the stairwell that led down from the kitchen to the basement acted like those old funnels and as a result, when you were in the basement you could hear what went on in the kitchen and I don't think that either Maxi or Merrily knew that. Usually, I don't pay much attention to what goes on upstairs when I'm in the basement, but I was down working on a project when I heard Maxi and Merrily come into the kitchen and they were talking as they walked in and I heard:

"....like you talking about him that way."

"I don't even know why you stay with him."

"I stay with him because I love him."

"Bullshit! If you loved him you wouldn't be such a slut."

"My personal life is none of your business young lady. Nothing that I'm doing is hurting that man and in fact when I get home I am so sex crazed I practically destroy him. I will not have him hurt Merrily and you had better understand that. And while we are on the subject, you will start to show him the respect that he deserves. I do not want you upsetting him. Do you understand me?"

There was a brief period of silence and then Maxi said again, "I said do you understand me?"

"Yes mother."

"Good. Now let's get dinner started."

Well, there it was. "You wouldn't be such a slut" and "nothing I am doing is hurting that man. In fact I am so sex crazed when I get home I practically destroy him" pretty much spelled it out to me at least. I had what I needed to justify hiring a detective and I pretty much knew where to point him. I knew what Maxi's work hours were and she was always home on time so whatever she was doing had to be done on her lunch hour.

But did I really want to hire a detective? Maxi's "I stay with him because I love him" came through loud and clear and her forceful "Nothing I am doing is hurting that man" did show some concern for me. I did find it interesting that Merrily knew what Maxi was doing while I hadn't had a clue, only a feeling. Maxi was loving and affectionate to me and God knows she gave me all I could handle in the bedroom. Maybe she was one of those women who no one man could satisfy. Whatever, I had it good and I decided that what I didn't know for certain wouldn't hurt me and I let it go.

Funny thing about humans; they are born with a brain that has a million little compartments that hold all kinds of things. One of those small compartments stores a thing called 'curiosity.' I was able to keep the door to that compartment closed for almost a year, but all the time curiosity was inside kicking and beating on the door demanding to be let out. It kicked so hard that the door came off its hinges and what had been stored in that compartment got out.

The PI report had it all. Dates, times, places and names. That's right, not name, but names. The names were all attached to men she worked with in her office and the times were all long lunches. Some of those lunches were pretty long and in fact some of them lasted all afternoon. I guess when your boss is one of the ones you are playing with, you can get away with doing that.

If it had only been one lover, things might have been different, but seven lovers was enough to make me visit a doctor. I tested clean at that moment, but the HIV results would be a while in coming back. One thing was clear to me however, and that was that with seven men dipping into the well sooner or later, the water was going to become contaminated and if I kept drinking from that well I was going to get sick.

During the year that curiosity had been trying to break down the door, Merrily was being her usual. She would only speak to me when spoken to; she would leave the room when I walked in and in general she let me know – silently – that she didn't care for me the least little bit. She never found a job that would pay her enough to get a place of her own and it didn't look like she ever would. Maxi paid for Merrily's divorce and her ex was ordered to pay alimony, but he never did and he eventually left town without leaving a forwarding address. It looked like I was going to be saddled with the spiteful cunt for the rest of my life.

I sat there and read the PI report for the fifth time as I thought about what I should do. I kept trying to tell myself that I should just let things be. My life was rolling along and things were good between Maxi and I so just don't rock the boat, but even as I had those thoughts I knew that I couldn't do it. Regardless of Maxi's saying that she loved me and that nothing she was doing was hurting me it just wasn't true. It didn't hurt me when I didn't know, but that wasn't the situation anymore.

Maxi was stabbing me in the back. She was hanging horns on me and that knowledge did hurt. Even though I hadn't known it at the time, she was humiliating me every time she took me with her to her company picnic, her company Christmas party or other company social functions and sat me down in the company of her lovers. She might not have thought of it that way, but it was nonetheless true.

My problem was that I was happy with my life. I was happy with Maxi. Even knowing what she had been doing I was still not wanting to end things, but I wasn't a guy who could sit and suffer in silence either. And then of course, there was the "tainted well" thing. If nothing else, that had to be addressed. I decided to approach the problem obliquely and see what would happen. If things could be worked out fine, if not and things cratered, so be it. I put the PI report in my desk, closed up my office and went home.

That night when we went up to bed, Maxi got on the bed naked, which was a sure sign that she wanted to play. I smiled and went to the nightstand and took out a condom and began to unwrap it.

"Why are you doing that? You know I can't get pregnant."

"Condoms have other uses besides birth control."

Maxi wasn't stupid and she understood right away what I'd just said.

"How long have you known?"

"About a year now."

"A year? You haven't used one of those during the year, so why now?"

"Because I thought that you just had a lover, but now I know different. One long-term lover I could take a chance on, but finding out that there are at least seven changes things. Makes me want to take precautions. I tested clean by the way and I intend to stay that way."

She didn't say anything; just lay there watching me roll on the overcoat. When I got on the bed she spread her legs wide and waited. When I pushed into her, she gripped me with her legs, dug her nails in my butt cheeks and hissed:

"Fuck me lover. That's it lover, just like that; fuck your whore lover, fuck your whore."

When it was over and I was sitting on the edge of the bed tying off the rubber she said:

"If you have known for a year, why haven't you done something about it?"

"Why rock the boat? Home life was fine; I had no complaints in the sexual department and you seemed to care for me so I let it be until my curiosity finally got the best of me and I hired a private detective to find out whom, when and where."

"I was so careful. How did you find out?"

"You and Merrily told me."

She looked at me blankly and so I told her about the 'feeling' that I'd had and how she and Merrily had confirmed things with their talk in the kitchen.

"You have known for a year and you did nothing? You didn't care that I was with other men?"

"Oh I cared all right, but I convinced myself that I had a good life so why screw it up. I did my best to try and ignore it, but eventually my curiosity drove me to hire a PI and I'm glad I did. Like I said, one long term lover didn't worry me too much, but once I found out that you had at least seven I had to take steps to protect my self."

"You were safe. They all knew each other and they all knew that if one of them gave me something that I would end up giving it to all of them. They policed themselves. They are all married and didn't want to be carrying any surprises home with them."

"You don't seem overly concerned that I know."

"Of course I'm concerned, Hank. I worked very hard at making sure that you would never find out what I was doing. I knew if you found out it would change things for us and I did not want that to happen. I love you and the last thing I wanted was to hurt you. But you do know now and I don't know what to do. I have no plan because it was never supposed to happen. I was so careful."

"Not careful enough. You should have remembered the last time, Max. I wasn't supposed to find out then either. Last time, it was an auto accident you hadn't planned for. If it hadn't have been the freakish way the stairwell acted as a noise funnel it would have been something else. It doesn't matter how hard you work at hiding something Max. Something that you have no control over or even know about will always trip you up."

"You know I don't like to be called, Max."

"Tough shit Max. Why Max? Why did you do it? What did I do that made you go looking somewhere else?"

"It wasn't anything that you did baby. You are super in bed and always have been."

"Then why Max? Just tell me why."

"I was after something that you couldn't give me Hank."

"You just said I was super in the bedroom."

"That had nothing to do with it lover. The one thing I could not get from you was the God-awful rush I got from cheating. The sex I got from the others didn't even come close to what I got from you, but the cheating gave me orgasms you wouldn't believe. I'd lie there and look up at whoever's turn it was and think, 'That's it, fuck my married pussy. Drive that cock into my cheating cunt' and I'd have one hell of an orgasm. I'd say things like 'You get off knowing you're fucking another man's wife, don't you?' and when they would say 'Yes you fucking slut, I do' I would cum buckets. It was the same when I ran around on you just after we got married. The rush, the charge, the high all came from knowing that I was cheating."

She stared at me in silence for several seconds and then asked, "So what happens now?"

"I don't know Max. I do doubt that you will ever hear the words 'I love you' come from me again, but as long as you are willing to keep sleeping with me and fucking me we can probably hang on."

"You want to make love to me even though I'm screwing other guys?"

"No Max; I won't be making love to you – I'll be fucking you – and you won't be screwing other guys anymore. Unless of course, you are lying to me."

"What does that mean?"

"You were only fucking them because of the charge you got out of cheating, right? It isn't cheating behind my back now that I know about it so since I know there won't be any – what did you call it, rush? – when you fuck them so unless you just lied to me there is no sense in doing it any more."

I waited a second or two and then said, "Why don't you go down on me and get me up again."

She looked at me as if I had two heads, grabbed her pillow and left the room. I watched her go, shrugged and went to bed.

When I got up in the morning, Maxine had already left for work and when I got home that night I found that she had moved out. She took everything of hers. Well almost everything; she left Merrily behind.

~~***~~

I made no attempt to find out where Maxine had gone and for the next week and a half, Merrily stayed out of my way. It probably would have been better for all concerned if she hadn't avoided me because during that time period, I felt more and more shit upon and a rage was building in me that was just looking for something to set it loose.

It was Merrily who did it.

I hadn't seen Merrily in the week and a half since Maxine split and then one evening she came into the living room where I was drinking beer and watching TV and in her usual snippy manner she said:

"I suppose that now mom isn't here to make you let me stay, you are going to kick me out."

Wrong thing to say and the wrong tone of voice to say it in. It was just enough to let the rage out and Merrily took the brunt of it.

"In the first place, your mother never made me do anything. I let you stay because even though you were a bitch most of the time, you were still family. But now that your mother is gone, we aren't a family anymore, are we? I won't throw your miserable ass out, but it will cost you to stay."

"Cost me what?"

"Glad you asked. Two things and you either do them or you get out."

"What two things?"

"Two things that you will absolutely hate, but they are the price of your room and board. First you, will go and put on nylons, garter belt, high heels and a sexy dress and then come back here and do a slow and sensual strip tease until you are naked except for the heels, stockings and garter belt. Then you will spread your legs as wide as you can and ask me to eat your pussy."

I looked at my watch. "It is now seven-ten. You have one hour in which to do those two things. Get them done by eight-ten or get out."

She stared at me for about a minute and then with a pure look of hatred at me, she turned and left the room. I smiled for the first time since I'd read the PI's report. Merrily would be packed and out of the house within twenty-four hours. I chuckled to myself as I imagined her throwing clothes in bags and boxes in her rush to get away from me.

I was working on a fresh beer, watching the TV and congratulating myself on ridding me of the bitchy cunt when I heard:

"Well?"

I looked over and saw Merrily standing there. She had on nylons and heels, a short skirt that came to about three inches above her knees and a low cut blouse. She looked hot! She looked sexy as hell! It was not supposed to be happening. She was supposed to hear my conditions, give me the finger and get the hell out of Dodge, but she stood there giving me the first hard on she had ever given me. I sat there stunned and didn't know what to say. She smirked at me and said in her usual bitchy tone of voice:

"You want I should start?"

I took a deep breath and said, "What kind of music do you want?"

"I don't need music to take off my clothes."

"Okay then; get with it."

She spun around a couple of times as she undid the buttons on her blouse and then she slid it off and tossed it in my direction. A couple of dips and twists and the bra landed at my feet. She had a very nice firm set of tits. Some spins, dips and a few other moves and the skirt was in a puddle around her ankles. A little kick and her skirt landed in my lap. All she had left on were her thong, hose, heels and garter belt. She danced over and stood in front of me.

"You want to take my panties off with your mouth?"

"No thanks; I want you to do it all."

She did a little shimmy, took off the thong and held it under my nose for a second and the dropped it in top of my head. She danced over to the easy chair, sat down, spread her legs wide and put them up on the chair's arms. She looked at me, smirked (she obviously knew the condition she had me in – rock hard) and said:

"Come on over here stud and eat my pussy."

I couldn't believe that she'd done it. She was not supposed to, but she did everything I told her to do. I just could not believe it. I just couldn't. I looked at her spread out and waiting for me to get up and bury my face in her pussy and I thought "what a waste." I got up and she smirked again. I didn't see if the smirk disappeared as I walked by her and said "Goodnight."

I went to my bedroom, undressed and took a shower (a cold one but it didn't help) and then got in bed. I propped myself up with a couple of pillows, took the book I was reading off the nightstand and tried to get back into it. I say tried because I was distracted. I still had the hard on that Merrily had given me and every time it started to go down I would think of her spread out in the easy chair and it would stiffen back up. After about an hour, I finally gave up trying and put the book down.

I was reaching over to turn off the bedside lamp when the door opened and Merrily walked in. She still had on the heels, hose and garter belt and she walked over to the bed and looked down at me.

"You didn't eat my pussy."

"I never said I would. I just said that you had to ask."

"You wanted to. I could see it on your face. You wanted to slip your tongue into me; you wanted to lick and suck my clit and taste me. You still want to. I can see the proof sticking up there. If you never intended to do it why did you make me go through with all of that?"

"You weren't supposed to do it."

"What? You expected me to say 'fuck you' and leave? And go where? I have no idea where mom is and I damned sure wouldn't go back to that faggot I divorced even if I knew where to find him. I don't make enough waiting tables at the café to get my own place. It was a no-brainer! If I want a roof over my head, I have to do what you want and right now what you want is to taste my pussy."

Before I could say anything, she caught me by surprise. She got on the bed, swung over me in a sixty-nine and pushed her pussy down into my face even as her mouth swallowed my cock. There is a time to protest and a time to fight to stop things, but that time is not when a hot mouth is working on your cock. I never had any intention of doing anything with her or to her, but there I was with my cock in her mouth and her hot, wet pussy on my lips. Add to that, I had been used to getting sex from her mother on an almost daily basis and I'd just gone almost two weeks without any and what was going to happen was a foregone conclusion.

I came rather quickly, but Merrily kept her mouth on me and kept working on me to get me up again. Meanwhile, my mouth was busy on her box and she was doing a lot of moaning so I must have been doing something right. When she was satisfied with what she'd built, she reversed herself, swung over me, impaled herself on me and started riding me. She came twice before I was ready and then I rolled her over on her back and pounded her pussy. I gave her one more orgasm just before I blew my load into her. I pulled out and fell to the bed next to her and then it hit me. I hadn't used a condom.

"Oh shit!" I muttered.

"What's wrong?"

"I didn't use a condom."

"So what? I'm on the pill."

"Why?"

"Why what?"

"Why did you just do what you did?"

"If I'm going to stay here, I'm going to have to pay my way." She reached down and started fondling my cock. "I've just paid part of today's rent and as soon as I can get some cooperation out of our little buddy here I'll pay the other half."

She did get cooperation from 'our buddy' and I ended up falling asleep exhausted. And that is how we ended up with me looking down at her in the moonlight.

~~***~~

She woke me up with a blowjob, which turned into a fuck session, and I went to work with a smile on my face for the first time in a while. Just as I was leaving the house, Merrily said:

"Your bed is so much more comfortable than mine. Unless you object I'm going to move into your room with you."

I just kind of nodded okay and left.

For the next week, Merrily did her best to fuck me blind. At least twice a night every night and she was wearing me out. She was a carbon copy of her mother – she was insatiable. It must have been in Maxi's genes and was passed on to her daughter. I asked her if she was trying to fuck me to death and she said she was only trying to build up her account. When I asked what she meant by that she said:

"Aunt Flo will be paying me a visit soon, so for a while I won't be able to pay the days rent so I'm trying to pay a little in advance."

The day Aunt Flo did arrive, Merrily had dinner ready when I got home from work and I managed to get the better part of a bottle of Merlot into her and I finally asked her how she went from hating me or despising me to being my bed buddy overnight.

"You were a man."

"Well, yeah."

"I didn't trust men. A couple of the men that mom brought home with her tried to do things with me when they woke up and she was still sleeping."

"Wait a minute. You were only six or seven when I started seeing your mom and she wasn't seeing other men while she was going out with me, was she?"

"No. It all happened before you."

"Oh God, you poor kid. What did your mom do about it?"

"Nothing, because I never told her."

"Why not?"

"I was afraid to. Don't ask me why I was afraid, because I don't know. Another time, a man offered me candy to get in his car and go for a ride with him. I ran away from him also. I got to where I was nervous around adult males. I stayed clear of them as much as I could. All of that transferred onto you. Mom brought men home and they tried to get me. Mom brought you home ergo you would try too."

"I never did anything like that."

"No, but I was waiting for you to. I just knew it was going to happen. Then things gradually changed and I started thinking that you were trying to take my mom away from me. We used to do all kinds of things together and when you came along we stopped doing stuff together. Again, you were the bad guy. I resented you being in our lives and it showed in my attitudes towards you. You would tell my mom things and I would get hollered at or punished so I blamed you.

"There was a whole lot more to it and it fed on itself. Things like my being sent to Mount Airey. They were some really fucked up kids there. I mean really fucked up kids. One girl used to piss in a glass and set it next to her bed in case she woke up thirsty in the middle of the night. Another kid would drop his pants and shit on the floor. Didn't matter where he was, he would drop and dump then he would stick his fingers in it and write stuff on the walls. I didn't belong in there with them, but I was there. I was there and I knew, just knew, that my mother would never have done that to me so it must have been you who made her do it. You couldn't do anything right in my eyes. Anything that was bad, anything that was wrong, was because of you."

"If men were bad why did you marry David?"

"David wasn't a man; David was a boy, a kid like me and I married him just so I could get out of the house and away from you. And boy did that turn out well. Living with David reinforced the idea in my head that the male of the species needed to be eliminated. Tom and Mark, the two next door neighbors, came over one day when David was gone. I guess they weren't pure homosexuals, probably were Bi, and told me to take my clothes off. They said David told them they could fuck me whenever they wanted. They grabbed me and started to take my clothes off of me, but I managed to grab a lamp and smash Tom in the head with it and when he went down, I went after Mark and he ran from the house. I told David about it when he got home and the asshole just looked at me and shrugged. It wasn't long after that that I caught him with Mark in his ass."

"I guess I can see why you didn't trust men."

"There's more. I moved back in here and I got the job as a waitress at the café and there wasn't a day that went by that some asshole didn't grab my ass when I walked by his table or try to cop a feel of my boobs when I bent over to put his food on the table. In short, as far as I was concerned all men were pigs.

"Not too long after that, I caught mom fucking around on you. Here you were, the man that she just loved so much, and she was fucking around on you. If she really loved you how could she do that? Bear in mind here that this is what was going on in my head, and we both know I was prejudiced against you anyway. Anyway, she is fucking around on you and not with just one man, but several so obviously she didn't really love you, but for some reason couldn't break away from you. She must have known that you were bad just as I did or she wouldn't be doing that."

"How did you know she was cheating on me with those seven guys?"

"Seven? I only know of three. I was downtown one day around lunchtime and I thought I drop in on her and have lunch with her. Just as I came up to her building, she came out with a guy. They were hand in hand and being curious, I followed along behind them. They went across the street to the Hilton, got a room and went up to the sixth floor. That made me even more curious so I was there at lunchtime the next two days and each day she went across the street to the Hilton with a different guy. That night I got on her about it, but she told me that it meant nothing, that she loved you but was just using them. I never did understand it."

"Well babe, that makes two of us"

"Bottom line, to me anyway, was that it just reinforced what I had always believed about you."

"So what changed?"

"What happened last night. When you gave me your conditions in my mind I went 'Aha! Just what I thought. Another fucking pig!' But a pig that I needed unless I wanted to move into a cardboard box under the 12th Street overpass. I sat in that chair, spread out for you, seeing the look on your face as you looked at my pussy and smiling inside at having been finally proved right about you. When you got up and moved toward me I was thinking, 'Come on motherfucker, I've waited years for the chance to prove that I was right and that you are a piece of shit like all the others.' When you walked by me and said goodnight I was stunned. It couldn't be. You had to eat my pussy. You just had to prove me right. But you didn't. I sat there in that chair for what must have been an hour trying to figure out what had just happened.

"I'm not sure why I got up and came into the room. No, that's not true. I came in here because I had gotten myself so horny doing that stupid dance that I needed to get off. I knew from the look on your face when I danced and then spread my pussy for you that you were just as horny and as much as I hated doing it, I was going to give you what we both wanted. I was surprised when you didn't get out of bed and grab me when I walked in. I saw your hard cock sticking up and you were a man, so you were supposed have your way with me. All the other men in my life had. But you just laid there looking at me."

"All the other men in your life?"

"I haven't been a virgin since I was twelve sweetie. I enjoyed the sex, but I could barely stand the boys and men who gave it to me. They got off and got me off, but they all treated me like dirt while they were doing it. But you just laid there and kept your hands to yourself. Be honest with me sweetie; if I had not have taken things in my own hands, would you and I be here now?"

"Honestly? No. Make no mistake honey, I wanted you – I wanted you bad – but you were Maxi's daughter and as such you were off limits. I would never have touched you on my own, but thankfully you took care of that."

"You do know that I was only going to use you to get myself off, right? But something happened. About half way into it I realized that it felt, I don't know, I guess the best way to say it is that it felt right. I didn't get much sleep that night. I laid there watching you sleep and wondered about what had just happened. I was thoroughly confused. I'd never felt that way before. I'm not talking about the orgasms, but the way I felt about the act itself. It was the first time I didn't want to just get up and leave when it was over. When you stirred in the morning and I woke you up with that blowjob it was the first time in my life that I had ever done something like that. And again, it just felt right. I don't understand it; it doesn't make any sense, but it felt right."

~~***~~

The next morning we went to the Village Inn for breakfast and over pancakes, Merrily suddenly said:

"She does love you."

"What?"

"My mom. She does love you. Always on me to make sure that I didn't upset you. Always hustling around to make sure that everything was just right for you when you got home. She never bought a piece of clothing without asking me first if I thought you would like it. I could never figure out, given the way she was always gushing about you, how she could screw all those other guys."

"As I said honey, that makes two of us."

"Kind of puts me between a rock and a hard place."

"Why?"

"Because she loves you and it is plain to see that regardless of what you say, you wish she was here."

"How is that a rock and a hard place?"

"Because I want my mom happy and that means back with you, but I'm happy with the way things are right now and I don't want it to stop. So here I am wanting her to come back, but not wanting her to come back and that's the rock and the hard place."

"I doubt you need to worry. She's been gone a month and hasn't bothered to try and get in touch with either of us."

"I wonder if something happened to her."

"Nothing as of last Thursday afternoon."

"How do you know that?"

"I called her at work a couple of times a week and when she answers, I hang up."

"Why don't you just talk to her?"

"She knows where we are if she wants to talk to us."

"If that's the way you feel, why do you bother to call?"

"To make sure that she is all right."

"That doesn't make any more sense than what mom was doing."

I didn't have an answer to that so I took another bite of pancake.

~~***~~

Another two weeks went by. Satisfied that Maxine was okay, I stopped calling her at work. She made no attempt to reach either Merrily or me and I had no idea what I would say if she did. I doubted very much that it would be "Hurry home, I've missed you" and I said as much to Merrily over dinner one night and she laughed and said:

"Right! That's why you kept calling to check on her."

Friday night when I got home from work and as soon as I was in the door I heard Merrily call out:

"In the living room, Hank."

Hank? She had always called me sweetie. Why the change? I walked into the living room and saw Maxine sitting next to Merrily on the couch. She gave me a nervous smile and said:

"Hello Hank."

"Hello Maxi."

"At least you didn't say 'hello Max.'"

"What brings you around after so long?"

"You probably won't believe it, but I missed you."

"You are right, I don't. How could you have time? A full time job and seven lovers should keep you so busy that you wouldn't have time to think of me."

"There aren't any lovers, Hank. I haven't been with a man since I left."

She saw the look on my face and said, "I don't blame you for not believing that, but it is true. I want to come home Hank."

"Why? I assume that you left because you didn't like the position I took when I found out about your seven bed buddies. That position hasn't changed any."

"What I want and what I'm asking for Hank is a chance to try and change it."

"Again, why?"

"Because I loved what we had. I know it was me who ruined it, but I was still happy with it and I would like the opportunity to try and get it back. I promise that if I get it back, I will never again do anything that will screw it up."

"Why in the world would you expect me to take another chance on you Maxine? Haven't you ever heard that saying, 'Fool me once, shame on you; fool me twice shame on me?'"

"Yes Hank, I've heard it, but I've also heard the one that says, 'Three strikes and you are out. I have two strikes against me, Hank and I don't want to be out so I'm not taking that third strike.'"

I was silent for a bit and then I took a deep breath and said, "It doesn't matter anyway, Maxine. There have been some changes since you left."

"I know and it won't be a problem."

"You know? How?"

"She told me."

I looked over at Merrily and she looked back at me and shrugged.

"How can that not be a problem?"

Merrily stood up, walked over to me and handed me the day's paper and then went back and sat down beside her mother and said:

"Turn to page three."

I opened the paper to page three and saw it was a full-page ad for a local furniture store. In bold letters across the top of the page it said:

"Three days only!" and the copy underneath read, "Every king sized bed must go. You can not beat these prices anywhere. With every king sold we will include a set of sheets, pillowcases and a comforter. Do not delay. Hurry down while we still have a large selection in stock. At these prices they won't last long."

I looked up from the page and looked over at Maxine and Merrily and they were both smiling at me.

And FYI – My parents still haven't tried to get in touch with me.

The End

Here is a preview of another story you may enjoy:

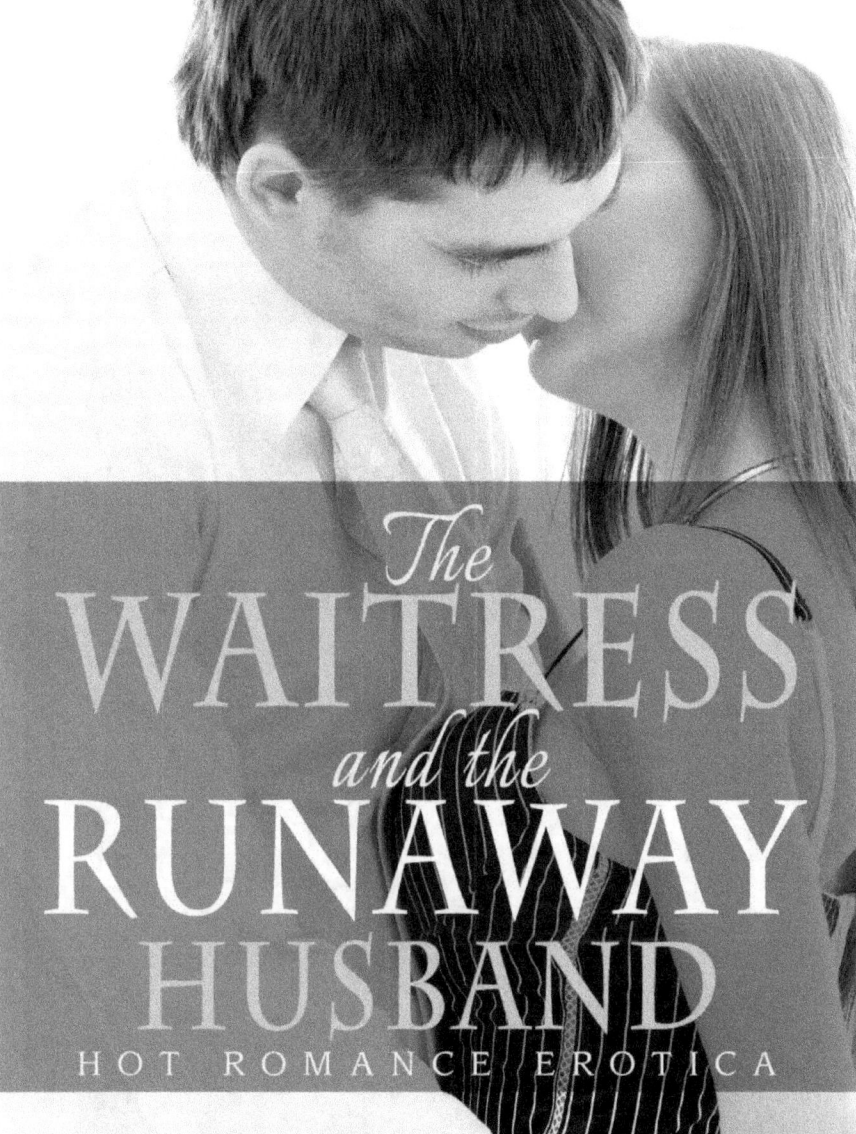

The
WAITRESS
and the
RUNAWAY
HUSBAND

HOT ROMANCE EROTICA

JUST PLAIN BOB

The sign read "Harpersville – 1 mile" and just beyond it another sign listed the restaurants and other services available at the exit. I needed gas and there was a Conoco station at the exit and I had a Conoco card so I pulled into the right lane and slowed for the exit.

As I filled the tank I looked around and saw that there was a restaurant across the street. It was a little early for supper, but what the hell, I already stopped. After I topped off I drove over to the restaurant and went inside. It had a nice 'homey' atmosphere and there were some nice aromas wafting through the place.

I took a seat in a booth and had no sooner sat down when an extremely attractive waitress came up, handed me a menu and asked:

"What would you like to drink hon?"

I smiled at the "hon" and thought *Don't I just wish I could be her honey.* I told her coffee with cream and when she went to get it I looked over the menu and settled on the liver and onions with mashed potatoes and green beans. The waitress, Joyce was the name on her tag, took my order and I watched her ass move in her jeans as she walked toward the kitchen to turn in my order.

It was a little early for supper so the place wasn't really busy, at least not busy enough to keep the two waitresses fully occupied. Joyce, apparently with nothing better to do, came over and said:

"I've not seen you in here before."

"Never been in here before. Just passing through."

"That seems to be the way it always is. The good looking guys are always just passing through."

"Pickings that slim around here?"

"Worse than slim. There are some nice looking guys, but almost all of them are losers. Only interested in hunting, fishing, car racing and drinking."

"Then why stay here?"

"Where would I go? I never finished high school so I doubt I could get a good enough job to be on my own. At least here I can still live at home."

"Good enough job? A good waitress can get a job anywhere. Most of the waitresses I knew back home did real well."

"I do okay here."

"Then you could do okay anywhere."

A bell rang and a voice called out "order up." And Joyce said, "That'll be you hon" and she headed for the kitchen. She was back in a minute with my meal. She left and came back a minute later and topped off my coffee cup. She walked through the place and topped off everyone else's coffee and then went back behind the counter where the cash register was.

I noticed as I ate that she was watching me. I wondered if maybe it might be to my advantage to linger a few days in Harpersville. I could make it to Rancho Mirage in two days and I didn't need to be there for another nine days. Joyce saw me finish my meal and she came over and asked me if I would like dessert and I took a pass on it. She started to leave and then she hesitated.

"You said that you were just passing through. Where are you headed?"

"Rancho Mirage in California. I have a job waiting for me there."

"California? I'd like to see California some day. I'm twenty-two years old and I've never been more than a hundred miles from this place."

"So go. Just pack your bags and go."

She had a wistful look on her face and I have no idea why I said it, but I looked into her eyes and said:

"Pack your bags, throw them in my truck and you can keep me company on the ride."

"I couldn't do that. What would I do when I got there? Where would I go? Where would I stay?"

"As for what you would do I've already told you that a good waitress can get a job anywhere. As for where you would stay you can stay with me until you find a place of your own. I'll be staying with my brother and his wife and they have plenty of room."

"You make it sound so easy."

"I don't know about easy, but I do know that you can sit around and wish for this or that, but you aren't likely to get it if you don't get off your butt and go for it."

She laughed and said, "That's true, but I don't know you. I don't know anything about you. For all I know you might be an axe murderer."

"I know just as little about you. For all I know there is a jealous husband watching us talk and he might be out in the parking lot waiting to kick my ass when I leave."

"No fear of that. There isn't a man living in this county I'd let myself be caught dead with."

"Tell you what. I don't need to be there for another nine days. I can stay over here for a day or two and you can get to know me better. Where is a good motel?"

"Take a left out of the parking lot and three blocks down on the left."

"What time do you get off work?"

"Nine."

"I'll pick you up at nine and we can go somewhere for a drink and get to know each other."

"You are serious?"

"Absolutely."

To purchase the book, look for **The Waitress and the Runaway Husband.**

Here is another preview of a story you may also enjoy:

THE MIND TALKER ROMANCE SERIES

AWARENESS

BOOK 1

DARLA DUNBAR

"So sexy…"

"God I'd love to do her…"

"I wonder if I could find that outfit in my size…"

Ananda had to fight laughter, curling an errant lock of dark auburn hair around her finger as she fought through the crowd of people around her. Laughing for no reason, at least none that could be seen by the general population, is typically frowned upon and usually makes finding friends much more difficult. This she had learned the hard way thanks to the cruelty of middle school students and their need to be popular. Still, it never ceased to surprise her how many inane thoughts humans regularly had running through their minds. Sometimes Ananda had to totally isolate herself in order to get a moment's rest, particularly when surrounded by the chatter from all directions. Her honey-colored eyes flitted back and forth as she scanned the mass of people around her, thoughts flying into her mind in rapid succession.

It wasn't like Ananda couldn't turn it off, her ability to hear other people's thoughts. When she was younger, it was definitely more difficult to sift through the roiling voices and images that seemed to seep into her head with little direction or effort. At first when her ability manifested at the tender age of eleven, Ananda was terrified as were her parents, who were ignorant of such abilities. Her older brother, Ryan, had been a source of strength and stability for her as the family went from one psychologist to another attempting to find a reason or cure for the 'voices' Ananda claimed to hear. It was he who helped her find a center in order to control the flow of voices until they were barely more than a brush against her mind. Ryan's move across the country for school was rough though manageable for Ananda as she began to explore the range of her ability and discover the fun she could have with it. Her moral compass wasn't as low as some, so she didn't use it for anything that would get her ahead academically, but she did use it to benefit herself and those she loved.

"Ananda, over here!"

Refocusing on the crowd around her, Ananda spotted one of the few people she could actually call a friend. Kerri wasn't what anyone would call quiet. Her small stature and pixie-like features made it seem as if she could be blown away by a single puff of air, but her exuberant personality and sharp, sometimes biting, use of sarcasm made her seem larger than her thin frame. Bright red hair the color of the sunset and eyes that seemed to change color depending on her mood completed the full package that was Kerri Donahue. However, it wasn't just Kerri's larger-than-life personality that drew Ananda in, it was more of what Kerri didn't exude. Her mind was quiet.

No matter how intently Ananda poked and prodded, she could only get a faint hum and vague feelings from her friend's mind. Rather than being unnerved by that, Ananda felt a sense of relief at finally finding one person who didn't give her a headache just by being around so often. Even with her brother Ryan, Ananda had to occasionally leave in order to calm her own mind and get some relief from his mind's 'voice.'

The fact that Kerri seemed oblivious to how special she was sometimes made Ananda pause and wonder if she was the only one out there with a strange ability. Was there someone out there like Professor X who was searching for people like her? Was there a way to find others? Or did she spend way too much time reading comic books and hoping that some parts of those stories were influenced by actual facts?

In the nine years since Ananda discovered her ability to read minds, not once had she ever come across anyone who seemed to be able to do the same. She had tried going to palm readers and calling so-called psychics, but so far they had all been scams. Their own minds would betray their lack of abilities sometimes before Ananda had even handed over her money. She had decided upon going to NYU with the vague hope that in a city as crowded as New York, there would be at least one other person who shared in her ability that she could commiserate with.

After two years of hoping and searching, she had grown discouraged and until meeting Kerri, Ananda had even considered moving back home to Phoenix and abandoning her search altogether. Meeting the other girl had been soothing to her soul and Ananda felt renewed enough to continue her search for others like her; she had even decided to expand her search overseas.

If you enjoyed this other sample, then look for: **Awareness by Darla Dunbar**.

Also by this Author:

The Prodigal Family: The Abbotts

Watching My Shared Wife

The Waitress and the Runaway Husband

Baiting Mr. Little

From the Author

If you enjoyed any of my books then please share the love and promote my books in Amazon.

If you write me a review and send me an email I will send you a free book, or many.
(Just know that these emails are filtered by my publisher.)

Good news is always welcome.

One Last Thing, For Kindle Readers...

When you turn the page, Kindle will give you the opportunity to rate this book and share your thoughts on Facebook and Twitter. If you enjoyed my writings, would you please take a few seconds to let your friends know about it? Because... when they enjoy they will be grateful to you and so will I.

Thank You!

An Open Letter from Just Plain Bob

A message for those who like my stories, those who hate my stories, those who are indifferent and those who have yet to make up their minds.

I have often stated that I really don't care what others think about my stories, that I write for my own enjoyment and then I offer to share. If you like my stories fine and if you don't, also fine since I have already satisfied my target audience - me!

It is human nature to strive to get better. If you take up bowling your first games are going low scoring, but you will work and practice to get better and as your average climbs you may forget the game where you had three gutter balls and shot an eighty-six, but that game is still there in your past.

Your first time on the golf course you shot an eighty on the front nine, but did you settle for that being your game or did you work to improve? You may eventually get a three handicap, but that nine hole eighty is still there as part of your past.

When you hired in at your job did you say, "Cool, I got it made" and do nothing more than what you barely had to do or did you go to work thinking that, "Someday I'm going to be running this place." You might never climb that high, but human nature says that you are going to at least try.

It is the same with authors who write stories and post them on sites like Literotica. Their first stories might not be all that good, but comments and feedback along with a desire to get better drive them toward putting out a better product or to at least try.

I'm no different. My first stories might not have been all that great, but they are still there on the hard drive. I like cheating wife stories and five years ago I found my first adult site that catered to cheating wife stories. It was a pay site, but it had a policy of giving a free lifetime membership to anyone who submitted five stories to the site. How hard can that be I said to myself as I sat down and fired up the word processor and went to work.

I sent my five stories in and sat back to enjoy my free membership and a funny thing happened. I started getting feedback, most of it positive, and I became hooked. I started cranking out more stories. The site I was sending my stories to had seven categories:

Bisexual
Cream Pie
Groups

I Watch
Gang Bang
Racial
SM/BD

I know nothing about bisexual or SM/BD and I had no interest in Groups so all the stories I wrote I tailored for the four remaining categories:

Cream Pie
I Watch
Gang Bang
Racial.

I turned out eight stories a month, two for each category, which means that after five years I have over 120 stories in each of those categories and they are all still on the hard drive.

A year ago I received an email asking me why I never posted stories on Literotica. The answer? I didn't know about Lit. I pulled it up, liked what I saw, and started sending in stories to it. All new stories? No, not hardly, not with over 400 stories sitting on the hard drive. Maybe one new story for each fifteen or so old ones. The newer ones are better, at least I think they are and I have received some feedback that leads me to believe that others think so too, and I will continue to write new ones.

But I am still going to recycle what is on the hard drive, stories that were written specifically to fit the four categories. That means that those of you who hate cream pie stories still have eighty or so to look forward to. Ditto for those who call me a racist; you will get another seventy or so interracial stories.

Those who hate wimps will only see about fifty more of those because the stories I sent to the I Watch category were split 50/50 between what some call wimps and some call "real men." Why the 50/50 split? It came from listening to the readers. I would get feedback asking me why all the men in my stories were hard asses. "In real life men are more forgiving, especially if it is the first indiscretion." So I would write stories with forgiving husbands and boyfriends and then the next batch of feedback would say, "Why are all your husbands spineless wimps" and I'd write stories that went back the other way.

Eventually I came to realize that I was wasting my time - there was no way I could write a story that would satisfy everybody and that is when I adopted my philosophy of writing for my own enjoyment and then offering to share.

As far as the gangbang stories? Well, what can I say? Gangbangs are gangbangs and there are still eighty or so of them to go.

The bottom line is that Literotica readers are going to see more of my old stories than my new ones. If I'm still around three or four years from now it will probably go the other way, more new than old.

I feel the need to respond to some of the comments and emails I have received. By far the largest percentage comes from people who say, "You are an asshole because all women are not whores and sluts and that's all you make them out to be."

Next most common is, "You must really hate women you sick fuck."

"You must be a wimp because all the men in your stories are wimps" is up there in the top ten along with, "Why don't you give it a rest and go crawl off in a hole somewhere."

There is a lot more, but I'm only going to address those four and in reverse order.

I won't stop and go crawl in a hole because I am enjoying the hell out of what I am doing and remember what I said, I am doing this for MY OWN ENJOYMENT and then I offer to share. Some obviously like my sharing with them and so I will continue to do so. No one is holding a gun to a reader's head and telling them they must click on a Just Plain Bob story or die. It is a conscious choice on the reader's part to move that mouse and click on that story.

When a man finds out he has a cheating wife or girlfriend there are only a limited number of ways he can handle it. If he loves her he can forgive, try to forget and try to hold on and somehow make things work. He can turn his back on her, walk away and get on with his life. The third option is to take revenge.

According to a good portion of those who send me feedback the first and second options are proof that the men are wimps. If the man takes the third option he is still considered a wimp if he doesn't do some sort of physical damage to the woman and her lover. These readers believe that the only way not to be a wimp is to kill, maim and destroy everything in sight. Doing that however, will invariably get the man throw in jail and that is why it so rarely happens in real life.

In real life most revenge takes place in the man's head when he says to himself, "I should have _____ (fill in the blank) the fucking cunt!" I know this because I have been there and done that (see The Dark Trilogy). In my stories I try to mirror real life so kill, maim and destroy are going to be for the most part absent. Outside of some fisticuffs there will be very little physical violence in my stories. Most of my husbands are going to do what I did, what several of my friends and others that I know have done, forgive, or walk away. If this makes them wimps and me a wimp for writing the story that way, so be it.

Next is the "I must hate all women." Nothing could be farther from the truth. I love women. I lust after women. I even like whores and sluts. I have been married four times, engaged two other times (that did not end in marriage) and I have always had girlfriends between marriages. My philosophy is that women were put on this earth for me to enjoy and I'm not talking just sexually. I could sit at the mall (and have) for hours and just girl watch.

The engagements, girlfriends and three of the four marriages bring me to the #1 anti JPB comment on the list.

"You are an asshole because all women aren't whores and sluts."

Well dear reader, you can not prove that by me! I will say up front that I KNOW all women aren't whores and sluts, BUT the majority of the women in my life were. My mother ran around on my father for years while he was driving a truck for a living. My Aunt Margaret cheated regularly on my Uncle Bill, as did my Aunt Mildred on my Uncle Paul. My Aunt Betty fucked around on my Uncle Bob for years and finally left him for his brother, my Uncle Wendell. Uncle Wendell in turn caught her on her knees at his company Christmas party giving Season's Greetings to his boss.

My sister is three times divorced and each divorce came about when the then current husband caught her out spreading pollen. Both of the engagements I mentioned ended when I found out that I was not the one and only and a lot of the girls I dated between marriages never made it to engagement status for the same reason.

And that brings me to my three ex-wives. The first one, Helen (I believe I commented on her in the intro to The Dark Trilogy) had seven different lovers before I found out what was going on. I was living proof that love is blind. Ditto with my second wife. She had a secret life that she hid from me and when I found out about her brother, his friends and the gangbangs she was history.

My third marriage ended in divorce because of a different kind of cheating (and I can just imagine the outrage I am going to get over this) - she cheated on me with an idea. I was away from home on business, she was lonely, a couple of Jehovah's Witnesses knocked on the door and my wife, with nothing better to do invited them in. When I came home from my trip I found out that she had found God. On a scale that runs from TRUE BELIEVER on one end to ATHEIST on the other you will find me just to the right of AGNOSTIC and since I would not allow myself to be SAVED the marriage eventually died.

So yes, I write about sluts and whores because as everyone knows, you tend to write about the things you know. And I do like sluts and whores, just not the ones that lie to me and cheat on me.

So be forewarned - if you click on a Just Plain Bob story you will be getting sluts, whores and husbands who do not kill, maim and destroy. There are other things you will rarely find in a Just Plain Bob story. Even though I try to mirror real life my stories all take place in StoryLand. In StoryLand STDs and unwanted pregnancies do not exist unless the author feels like they may add something to the story. Bad things do not happen in StoryLand unless the author so wills it and no amount of "You should have…" in comments and feedback will change a story already posted.

Lastly, I will touch on a truth. None of what I have written here means shit because the same readers will still read the same stories that they profess to hate and make the same comments they have always made. Knowing this, I will deliberately post stories that will have them frothing at the mouth.

It is the least I can do for an adoring public.

Thank you!

Just Plain Bob
justplainbob@awesomeauthors.org